DISNEY · PIXAR

D1625552

∽ **BOOK NINE** ∽

DISNEP PRESS

New York · Los Angeles

Carl Fredricksen wanted to be an explorer. His hero was the legendary explorer Charles Muntz.

Carl's best friend was a girl named Ellie. The two dreamed of going on great adventures.

One day, Ellie showed Carl her adventure book. Inside was

a picture of Paradise Falls. Ellie made Carl promise to take her to
Paradise Falls one day.

"Cross your heart," she told him.

Carl crossed his heart. He was certain that he and Ellie would
have many adventures together.

When Carl and Ellie grew up, they got married. Carl sold balloons from a cart, and Ellie took care of animals at the zoo. They were very happy together.

Carl and Ellie tried to save money for a trip to Paradise Falls, but they could never collect quite enough.

Many years went by. Ellie passed away, and Carl grew lonelier and lonelier.

Then one day a boy named Russell knocked on Carl's door. Russell was a Junior Wilderness Explorer. He wanted to help Carl so that he could earn his Assisting the Elderly badge.

Carl didn't want Russell's help. To get rid of him, he asked the boy to find a made-up bird called a snipe.

Not long after that, Carl received some bad news. He was being sent to live in a retirement home. Carl was sad. All his memories of Ellie were in his house.

Remembering his old promise to Ellie, Carl came up with a plan. He tied thousands of balloons to his house and set sail for South America.

"We're on our way, Ellie," he said happily.

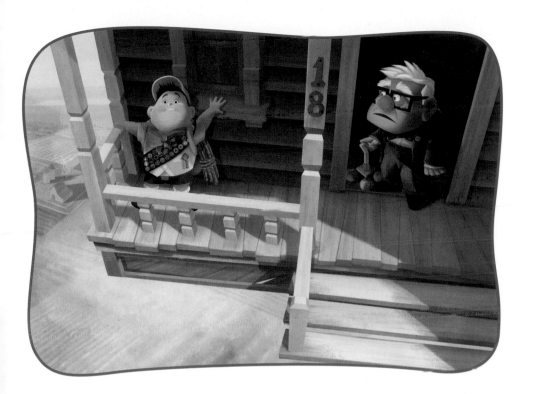

As the house flew over the city, someone knocked at the door. Carl was confused. He was thousands of feet above the ground. Who could be knocking?

It was Russell! He had been looking for the snipe under Carl's porch when the house lifted off.

"Please let me in!" Russell begged.

Carl had no choice. He let the boy inside.

Carl planned to let Russell off in the next town, but he never got the chance. The house flew into a storm. In no time at all, they had landed in South America.

Carl was thrilled to discover that they were just a few miles away from Paradise Falls.

"We could float right over there!" he cried.

There was just one problem. Once they left the house, they couldn't get back inside. The house was too high off the ground!

Then Russell had an idea. They could walk the house to the falls.

Russell and Carl made harnesses from the garden hose and set out for the falls, pulling the house behind them.

Along the way, Russell met an enormous bird. He named it Kevin. Kevin liked chocolate. He liked Russell, too.

Russell wanted to keep Kevin. As they set out for Paradise Falls again, he left a trail of chocolate for the bird to follow.

Russell and Carl hadn't gone far when they met a talking dog named Dug.

"My master made me this collar so that I may talk," Dug explained. Dug had been sent on a mission to find the bird. He tried to capture Kevin, but the bird was too big.

Kevin was following Carl and Russell, so Dug followed them, too.

When Carl and Russell woke up the next morning, Kevin was gone. The adventurers were about to start on their way again when three fierce dogs burst from the bushes.

The dogs were part of Dug's pack. When they found out that Dug had lost the bird, they insisted on taking Carl and Russell back to their master.

The dogs led Carl and Russell to a huge cave. Inside,
Carl got a surprise. The dogs' master was Charles Muntz, his
childhood hero! Muntz had been in South America all these
years.

The explorer invited Carl and Russell aboard his airship,
the *Spirit of Adventure*.

Muntz told Carl and Russell about his search for the Monster of Paradise Falls. As Muntz talked, Carl realized the "monster" was Kevin!

When Muntz found out that the bird had been following Carl and Russell, he became angry.

"Get them!" he told his dogs. Suddenly, Kevin swooped in. The bird picked up Carl and Russell and flew out of the cave.

Muntz tracked them down in his ship. Angry, he set Carl's house on fire.

Carl couldn't let his house go up in smoke. As he ran to beat out the flames, Muntz's dogs grabbed Kevin and dragged the bird onto the airship.

Russell was horrified. "You gave away Kevin!" he accused Carl.

Carl felt terrible, but he didn't know what to do. "I didn't ask for any of this," he told Russell.

Carl pulled the house the rest of the way to the falls without Russell's help. He'd finally kept his promise to Ellie. But he still felt sad. He wished Ellie could have been on the adventure with him.

Inside his house, Carl found Ellie's adventure book. He flipped through the pages. They were full of photos of their life together! At the end was a message from Ellie. It read THANKS FOR THE ADVENTURE. NOW GO HAVE A NEW ONE.

Carl realized that Ellie had gotten her wish after all. Their life together had been an adventure.

Suddenly, Carl heard a noise up on the roof. It was Russell!
He had stolen a bunch of balloons and was going to save Kevin.

Carl tried to follow, but without the balloons, his house was
too heavy. Carl had kept his promise to Ellie. Now he had to
keep his promise to Russell. He pushed everything he owned
out of the house until it was light enough to fly.

Carl caught up to Russell and together they fought Muntz. But Muntz tried to take over the house.

When Carl saw Kevin, he pulled a chocolate bar from his pocket. Kevin leaped for the chocolate, pulling Russell and Dug onto the airship with him.

Muntz wasn't so lucky. His foot caught on Russell's balloons and he drifted away.

Carl, Russell, and Dug flew Kevin home in the *Spirit of Adventure*. It turned out Kevin was a she—and a mom! Thanks to the adventurers, Kevin was reunited with her babies.

After a visit with the adorable chicks, it was time for Carl, Russell, and Dug to leave.